BibleRhymes'
NOAH AND THE ARK

K.W. McCardell & Antonella Chirco

BibleRhymes Publishing, LLC
Shelby Township, Michigan

Published and distributed by BibleRhymes Publishing, LLC.

ISBN-13: 978-0-9790605-1-9
ISBN-10: 0-9790605-1-6

LCCN: 2007906566

BibleRhymes' Noah and the Ark is Book 2 in the BibleRhymes series.

Printed in the USA
First Edition

10 9 8 7 6 5 4 3 2 1

Attention churches, schools, bookstores, and others:
Quantity discounts are available for fundraising, educational, and retail purposes. Please visit www.BibleRhymes.com for details.

Editing and typesetting by Steve McCardell.
Cover design by Mario Dominguez.
Art, including cover art, by Antonella Chirco.
Production coordinated by Kenneth McCardell.

BibleRhymes Publishing, LLC
Shelby Township, Michigan
www.BibleRhymes.com

Dedications:

To Russell William – this one's for you.
                    K.W.

*To my Dad, Mom, Vitina, Michele, Valeria, and Daniela, because my journey
with them has been just like an ark full of cute little animals, suprises, joy,
love, and lots and lots of fun!*
                    A.C.

Ages ago, people were bad.
The Lord looking down began to feel sad.

Try as some had to do what they should,
Too many didn't know how to be good.

God couldn't believe; He grieved in His heart.
He'd given the planet a wonderful start.

The world torn apart was a heartbreaking sight,
But God found a man who brought Him delight.

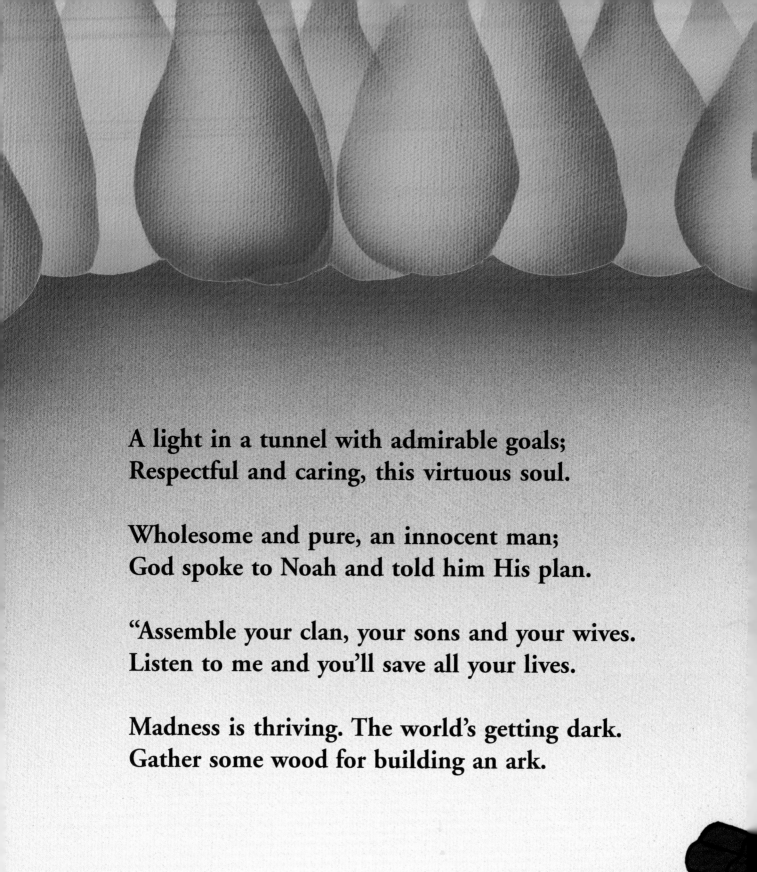

A light in a tunnel with admirable goals;
Respectful and caring, this virtuous soul.

Wholesome and pure, an innocent man;
God spoke to Noah and told him His plan.

"Assemble your clan, your sons and your wives.
Listen to me and you'll save all your lives.

Madness is thriving. The world's getting dark.
Gather some wood for building an ark.

"The spark that I needed, you've walked in My ways.
You're the colorful spot outshining the grays.

For forty whole days and forty whole nights,
Floods will submerge all that's in sight.

But you'll be alright: just build up that boat,
Pitch it with tar and use a good coat.

Then it will float, don't have any doubt.
Use gopher wood — it's wonderfully stout."

Touting his plan, the Lord didn't slow,
Explaining to Noah the things he should know,

Showing just how the boat should be made
With three different floors and rooms giving shade.

Noah obeyed, with God at his side.
The Lord was his shepherd and comforting guide.

Without any pride and without hesitation,
Noah launched into the boat's preparation.

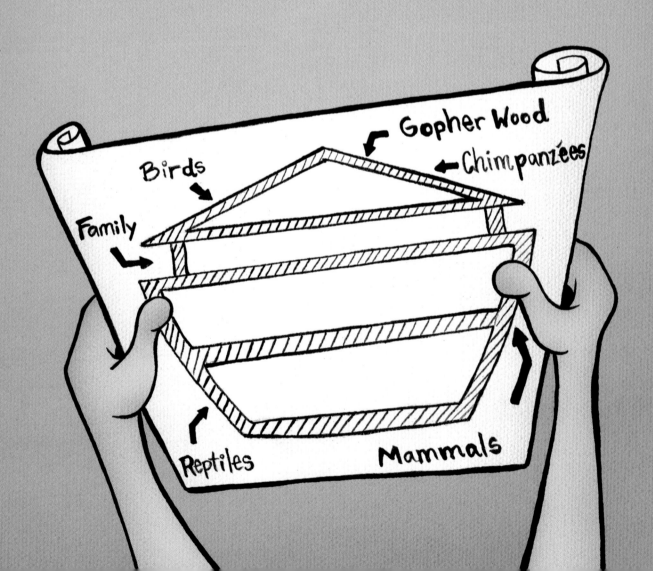

With patience his virtue, he got it all done
Enjoying the help of his wife and their sons.

He stood in the sun when done with the chore.
Then God whispered to him, explaining some more:

"Before you board up, there's more you should do.
Gather all creatures and group them by two.

Emus and zebras, hippos and bears,
Even some goats with shaggy long hair.

"There will be more, like cattle and dogs;
High jumping bunnies and ribbitting frogs;

Big happy hogs — the boisterous kind;
Scour the earth and bring what you find.

"But don't get behind, there are seven days more.
Then it will thunder, lightning, and pour.

From eagles that soar to owls that fly,
Get seven of each of the birds in the sky.

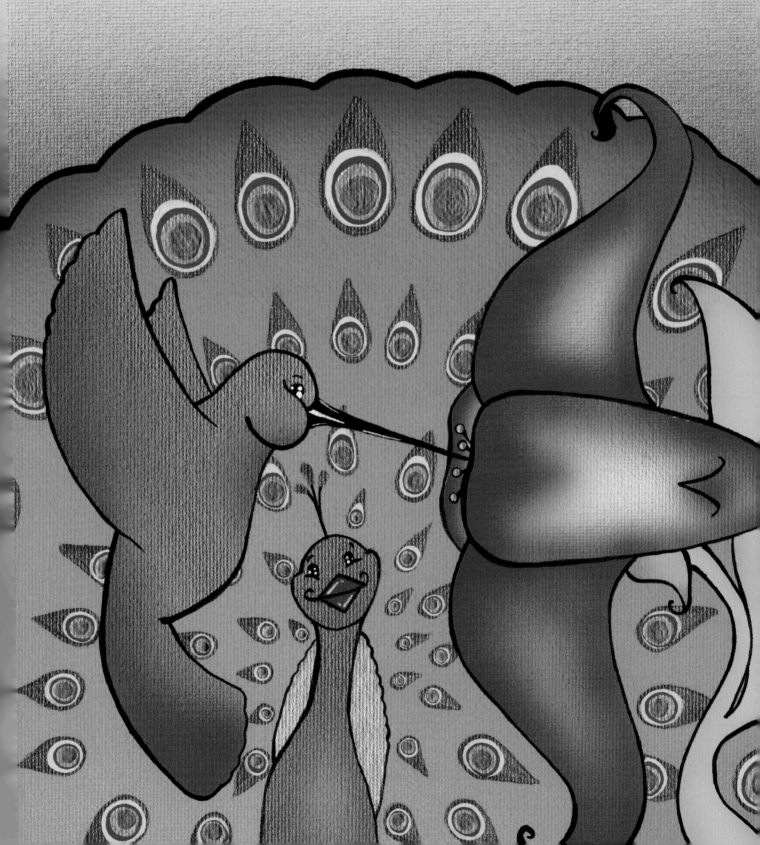

"Try to remember: this makes Me so sad.
My heart breaks in half that people turned bad.

I'm glad that I met you; you are a good friend.
Our bond has been formed and won't ever end.

You're welcome to spend forever with me.
My house is in heaven, the best place you'll see."

Noah, he listened and did what God asked.
Gathering animals sure was a task.

Basking in sun were lions and snakes.
He got rather nervous — was this a mistake?

No time for a break, he gathered them all
Whether they walked or slithered or crawled.

He called to his family, they came to his aid
By lining the animals like a parade.

Their beauty displayed, a marvelous sight.
A vision to dream of. What a delight!

All seemed alright and time for the ride.
The animals started heading inside.

The ramp plenty wide, they used it like stairs
With animals walking, grouped into pairs.

Hair being shed garnished the floors.
Noah, still working, fastened the doors.

A chimpanzee's snores caught him off guard,
As Noah stood near it, within just a yard.

Laughing so hard, he went to lie down.
Then came an ear-splitting, thundering sound.

Pounding rain fell, lightning was flashing.
Rivers were rushing with white-water splashing.

Crashing waves came; the ark got its test.
It kept them secure like eggs in a nest.

Needing a rest, Noah felt weary.
His eyelids were sagging; his vision was bleary.

Sleep made him cheery, he woke with a smile.
A cruise with a zoo, he relished this style.

While he had slept, the earth disappeared.
Now he was boating and stroking his beard.

He peered out a window, entranced by the view.
With land under water, the old world was through.

Then lightning struck too, shocking the sky.
He felt so relieved that his family was dry.

He let out a sigh and scratched on his head.
His nights would be spent on a turbulent bed.

The good Lord had said that he'd make it through.
His family and animals, they'd make it too.

Keenly he knew just what was at hand.
People were cleared from off of the land.

And it was clear why God brought the rain.
It wasn't to hurt or cause any pain.

People, insane, were bathing in sin,
Swimming in evil, diving right in.

Beginning all over with Noah's whole crew,
God felt secure. He knew what to do.

The earth would be new, with unblemished ground.
No pounding of hammers, no cities around.

The sound of the rain continued for days.
Then finally one morning, the sun brought its rays.

The gray of the sky was replaced by a blue.
Wind started blowing, the waters subdued.

Needing a clue, Noah sent out a dove.
It left from the ark and circled above.

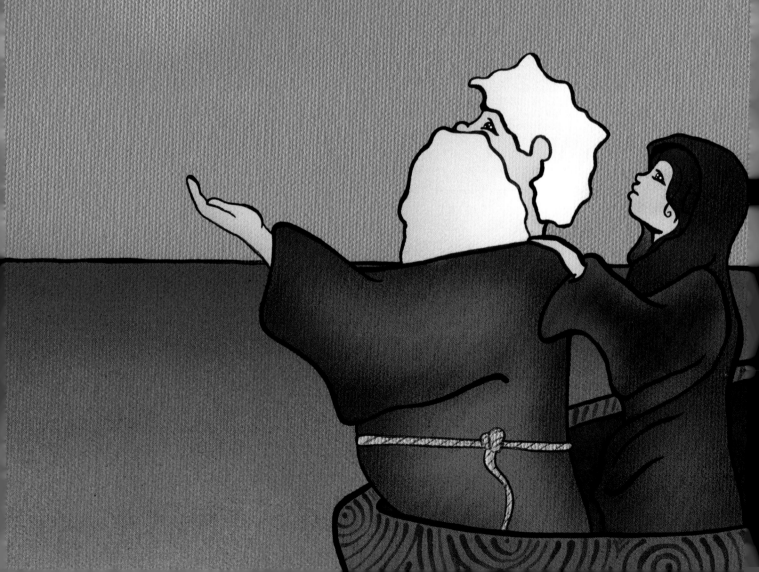

He watched it with love, it flew out of sight.
With no land around, it came back that night.

Right when it landed, it heard Noah say,
"You need to be leaving in seven more days."

The dove flew away when seven days passed,
Looking for land with wings flapping fast.

At last it returned with something to see,
Flaunting an olive leaf plucked from a tree.

Noah felt free, excited no doubt.
His joy overwhelmed him; he let out a shout.

The ark turned about and headed toward land.
Noah imagined his feet in the sand.

And soon they scraped bottom; the ark ran ashore.
His family all safe, he couldn't want more.

He opened the doors and let down the ramp.
The evening was coming. He had to make camp.

The animals scampered, sea-legs and all.
After months on a boat, they still didn't fall.

Hauling their gear, Noah's family left too.
They'd always remember the ark like a zoo.

Before Noah knew, God came as a friend.
He promised this never would happen again.

Men would be safe, He said it out loud.
Then a rainbow appeared way up in the clouds.

ABOUT THE AUTHOR:

Ken McCardell grew up in Royal Oak, Michigan, the youngest of five children. He went to a Christian elementary school, where the seeds of faith were planted.

Beginning in 2002, Ken spent several years as the manager of a cattle ranch in Montana, transitioning it from conventional to organic and humane production methods. While in Montana, he began writing poetry, which eventually took a spiritual turn and became today's BibleRhymes.

ABOUT THE ARTIST:

Antonella Chirco's passion for the visual arts came during her childhood years in Sicily. Born in Carini, Italy, in 1982, Chirco studied the arts in Palermo at the Liceo Artistico Statale Eustachio Catalano where she graduated in 2000. It was there that she experimented with ceramics, acrylics, oils, glass painting, crafts, and graphic design.

Chirco created glass paintings and sold them at local art festivals and craft shows. Her first public project was completed in 2003. It consisted of designing and painting the logo and name on the structure of a popular Sicilian restaurant.

Chirco moved to the United States in 2002. Since then she has painted in children's rooms, has created a number of acrylic on canvas paintings, and has completed the illustrations for her first book with BibleRhymes. Chirco is currently working on upcoming books for BibleRhymes.